Usborne English R
Level 3

Romeo and Juliet

Retold by Mairi Mackinnon
Illustrated by Simona Bursi

English language consultant: Peter Viney

You can listen to the story online here:
www.usborneenglishreaders.com/
romeoandjuliet

Contents

Romeo and Juliet are two young people from enemy families in the city of Verona: the Montagues and the Capulets.

Benvolio   Lord and   Romeo   Juliet   Lord and   Tybalt
            Lady Montague   Montague   Capulet   Lady Capulet

The two families hate each other…
and then Romeo and Juliet fall in love.

The words shown like this are taken directly from the play.

The market was a mess. Spoiled fruit and vegetables lay everywhere. One man was lying on the ground, and there was blood in the street.

"Another fight?" The Prince of Verona looked over the angry, silent crowd. "Lord Montague, Lord Capulet, this quarrel must stop. From now on, anyone from your families who starts a fight will pay with his life. Capulet, come with me. Montague, I'll see you later this afternoon. Everyone else, go home."

Montague turned to his wife. "At least Romeo wasn't here. Has anyone seen him?"

"I met him this morning, sir," said a younger man. It was Romeo's cousin, Benvolio. "He was out walking early. He seemed upset."

"He's been behaving strangely recently," said Montague. "I wish I knew why. He won't tell us anything. Benvolio, find out if you can."

Montague and his wife left, and the market place was quiet. Then a sad-looking young man came into the street.

"Good day to you, cousin," said Benvolio.

"Good? If you say so," Romeo answered.

"What's the matter? Are you in love again?"

"Yes, but she doesn't love me," said Romeo. "Rosaline's the most beautiful girl in Verona, but she says she'll never marry."

"Oh, Romeo, forget about her. She isn't the only girl in the city."

"You don't understand, Benvolio. You can't compare anyone else with Rosaline."

"Well, maybe you should try. Listen, there's a party at Capulet's house tonight. Rosaline will definitely be there, and there'll be plenty of other pretty girls too."

"At Capulet's house? Benvolio, we can't go there!"

"Of course we can. We'll wear masks. Nobody will recognize us. Come on, it'll be good for you, Romeo."

"Juliet, dear? Your mother's here."

"Thank you, Nurse." Lady Capulet came into the room and sat down. "Juliet, your father and I have decided. It's time for you to get married."

"Get married? But Mother, I'm not old enough."

"Don't be silly. Plenty of girls your age are married already. Count Paris has asked to marry you. He'll be an excellent husband."

"Count Paris? Oh, Juliet, he's a lovely man," said her nurse. "So handsome, so polite, and the Prince's cousin too!"

Verona's summer hath not such a flower.

"He's coming to the party tonight," said Juliet's mother. "You'll like him, I'm sure. Come with me, now. The first guests are arriving."

"Put your masks on, boys, and your dancing shoes," said Mercutio. Romeo and his friends were getting ready.

"No dancing shoes for me, Mercutio," said Romeo. "I'll just watch."

"He's in love," Benvolio explained.

"In love?" Mercutio laughed. "Oh, Romeo, don't be so dull!"

"Come on, boys," said Benvolio. "We'll miss all the dancing if we don't hurry."

In the Capulet house, the servants were taking away the supper tables, and the music was beginning. The Montagues arrived during the first dance, and everyone joined the dancers except Romeo. He couldn't see Rosaline anywhere.

Suddenly he looked much more interested.

"Who's that beautiful girl?" he asked a servant. "She's the brightest light, the richest jewel here. Everything else looks dark and dull and heavy beside her."

Someone had heard him. "That's a Montague voice," said Juliet's cousin, Tybalt. "How dare they come here? Where's my sword?"

"Tybalt, my boy, what's the matter?" asked Juliet's father.

Tybalt explained angrily. "It's Montague's son, Romeo. I'll kill him for this!"

"You will not," said Capulet. "I won't allow swords and fighting here. Take your quarrel somewhere else."

The dance ended, and Juliet went to the side of the room, where Romeo was waiting for her. He took Juliet's hand, and she looked startled.

"My hands are too rough for yours," he said. "Forgive me." He kissed her hand instead.

Juliet smiled. "I don't need to forgive you. You've done nothing wrong." Another dance had started, and no one was watching. Juliet and Romeo talked and talked. Then they kissed, once and then again.

"Juliet, dear? Your mother is asking for you,"
said the nurse. Juliet hurried away.

"Who is that lady?" Romeo asked.

"Who is she? Ha, that's Lord Capulet's
daughter! He'll be a lucky man, the one who
marries her!" She didn't notice Romeo's
horrified face.

"Come on, Romeo, everyone's leaving," said
Benvolio. "You've missed all the fun."

Now the nurse looked horrified. "Romeo
Montague? Oh, how shall I tell my Juliet?"

His name is Romeo, and a Montague.

The Capulet house was dark. The garden was cool, and the street outside was quiet. Romeo's friends had gone home.

A light appeared at a window, and someone stepped out onto the balcony. "Bright as the sun, my Juliet," said Romeo, "brighter than the morning."

That which we call a rose
By any other name would smell as sweet.

"Romeo!" said Juliet. She didn't realize that he could hear her. "Why must you be Romeo? Names mean nothing. A rose is still a rose, whatever its name. Change your name, change your family – or I'll change mine, so that we can be together."

"Change my name? I would do that for you," said Romeo. "Give me a new name, and I'll never be Romeo again."

"Oh, my sweet, how did you come in here? The garden walls are so high, and it's so dangerous for you!"

"How can a stone wall stop true love? I'm afraid of nothing, unless you're angry with me. If you look kindly at me, nothing can hurt me."

"You know how I feel about you already," said Juliet. "Oh, this is so sudden. How can I be sure that your love will last?"

"I promise you my love for ever, if you promise yours," said Romeo.

"I'd promise that again and again," said Juliet. "The more love I give you, the more I have for you. I'll send a messenger to you tomorrow. Tell me where to meet, and we can be married. Oh! I want you to go, and be safe, but then I want you to come back again... No, go, my love, good night."

Friar Laurence was collecting herbs in his small garden. He used them to make all kinds of medicines.

"Romeo! You're up early – or else you haven't slept at all."

"You're right about that," said Romeo dreamily.

"Are you still lovesick for Rosaline?"

"Rosaline? No, Friar. That wasn't love. I didn't understand true love until I met Juliet Capulet. Please, Friar, we want you to marry us."

"Well, this is a sudden change! But it could be a good thing, if it ends the quarrel between your families at last. Yes, I'll do it. Come back with Juliet this afternoon."

Benvolio and Mercutio were talking in the street. "So Romeo didn't come home at all last night?"

"He didn't, and he's made an enemy. Tybalt is looking for him."

"That's bad news. Tybalt is dangerous, and he knows how to fight." They saw Romeo. "Hey, what happened to you?"

Here comes Romeo, here comes Romeo!

"I'm sorry, friends. I needed to talk to someone."

"You needed to *talk*?" Mercutio laughed. "Well, you certainly look happier. Wait, who's this?"

Juliet's nurse hurried towards them. "I'm looking for Romeo. I have a private message for him." Mercutio and Benvolio left.

"I want to be sure that you're serious, young man," said the nurse. "My Juliet is so young. If you break her heart, I'll never forgive you."

"I'm serious, I promise you," said Romeo. "Tell Juliet to come to Friar Laurence's house this afternoon, and we can be married. Oh, I wish it was this afternoon already!"

Soon he was with Friar Laurence again, hand in hand with Juliet. "I hope this marriage will be a long and happy one," said the friar.

The city streets were hot in the afternoon sun. "We should go home," said Benvolio nervously. "This is fighting weather, and the Capulets are in town."

"Too late," said Mercutio. Tybalt and some other Capulet men were at the end of the street.

"We're looking for Romeo. Hey, you're his friend, aren't you?" shouted Tybalt. At that moment, Romeo arrived. "You're the one I'm looking for. Take out your sword and fight like a man!"

"Tybalt, I have no quarrel with you. You're almost family to me now," said Romeo. "Remember the Prince's law. Let's have peace here."

"Family? What do you mean?" Tybalt pointed his sword at Romeo.

"Romeo, won't you fight for yourself?" Mercutio took out his sword, and Tybalt rushed towards him.

"Benvolio, help me!" Romeo tried to separate Mercutio and Tybalt, but Tybalt reached past him and stabbed Mercutio. The Capulets all ran away.

"I'm dying," groaned Mercutio. "Your two families' stupid quarrel has killed me."

"Surely you can't be so badly hurt?" said Romeo.

Help me into some house, Benvolio.

"It's bad enough. Help me off the street, boys. Go and find a doctor." He groaned again and closed his eyes.

"It's too late," said Benvolio quietly. "He's dead, Romeo."

"It's my fault," Romeo said miserably. "Look, here's Tybalt again. I suppose he's proud of what he's done. My friend is dead because of you!" he shouted.

"Ha! I'll kill you next." Tybalt laughed nastily. Romeo ran forward. Tybalt wasn't expecting the attack. He fell back as Romeo's sword stabbed him.

"Romeo, you need to hide!" said Benvolio. "The Prince's soldiers are coming. If you want to save your own life, you can't stay here!" Romeo took one horrified look at Tybalt's body. Then he ran.

Soon there was a crowd in the street – Montagues, Capulets and the Prince himself.

"Who began this wicked fight?" The Prince's voice was like thunder.

"Sir, I can explain everything," said Benvolio. "Tybalt killed your cousin Mercutio, and now Tybalt is dead, too."

"Tybalt!" Lady Capulet started crying noisily. "My brother's own son! Prince, the Montagues must pay for this, a life for a life."

The Prince turned to Benvolio. "Tell me more."

"Romeo was trying to stop the fight, sir, but Tybalt wouldn't listen. Romeo couldn't stop him from killing Mercutio. Then Tybalt came back, and he was going to kill Romeo too. I've never seen Romeo so angry."

"Don't listen to him!" Lady Capulet shouted. "He's a Montague!"

Romeo must not live.

"Be reasonable, sir," said Romeo's father. "Maybe my son was wrong to attack Tybalt – but remember, Tybalt started the fight. Your law would punish him with death."

"That doesn't excuse Romeo," said the Prince coldly. "He may live, but he must leave the city and never come back. If he's seen here again, he must die."

Juliet walked nervously around her room. "Oh, when will it be dark? Then Romeo can visit safely."

Juliet's nurse came in. She was so upset that she could hardly speak. "Dead! Romeo, how could you do it?"

Juliet was pale with shock. "Romeo has killed himself? Then I have no reason to live."

The nurse didn't hear her. "Tybalt, my young friend! I can't believe you're dead!"

O Tybalt, Tybalt, the best friend I had.

"Tybalt and Romeo? Both of them?" whispered Juliet.

Her nurse understood her mistake at last. "No, my sweet. Tybalt is dead. That criminal Romeo killed him, and the Prince is sending him away from the city forever."

"Don't call him a criminal!" Juliet said angrily. "He's my husband, and now I'll never see him again. I wish I was dead!"

"Hush, my dear. I know where he is. I'll take a message to him, and I promise you'll see him again before he leaves the city."

Romeo was hiding at Friar Laurence's house. The friar had just come back. "It's not as bad as you think, Romeo. The Prince will let you live, but you must leave the city."

"Leave the city, and leave Juliet? That's worse than death! I'll never see her lovely face again!"

"Listen to me –" the friar began, but Romeo was lying on the ground, groaning. "Someone's coming!" the friar said, but Romeo didn't hear.

The visitor was Juliet's nurse. "Juliet is just the same," she told the friar. "Nothing can comfort her." "Stand up!" she said to Romeo. "If you love her, listen to me."

Romeo looked up. "Does she hate me?"

"She just lies on her bed, crying and crying," said the nurse. "Sometimes she calls out your name, and sometimes Tybalt's."

Romeo pulled out a knife, and was going to stab himself. "Stop that!" said the friar. "You've killed Tybalt already. Do you want to kill yourself now? Then Juliet will kill herself, too. Think, man! Juliet loves you. Tybalt tried to kill you, but you're alive; and the Prince has chosen not to kill you. Be grateful for that."

"You have a chance to see Juliet one last time," he continued. "Don't stay too long, but go to the city of Mantua. We'll speak to the Prince, and in time he may forgive you. We'll share the news of your marriage, and I do believe you can come back to the city and live happily. We'll send news, Romeo. Don't lose hope."

"Thank you, Friar," said Romeo. "That's true comfort. Let me say goodbye to Juliet, and tell her all this."

Tis very late. She'll not come down tonight.

Count Paris was visiting the Capulets.
"I'm sorry," Lord Capulet told him. "We
haven't been able to speak to Juliet about the
marriage yet. She loved her cousin Tybalt. She has
been crying in her room since she heard the news."

"I understand," said Paris. "Please, give her
my good wishes. I'll come back another time."
He stood up to leave.

"Wait," said Capulet. "She's a good daughter.
I know she'll do as I say. My wife will see her
before she goes to bed. We'll tell her she's going
to marry you on — what day is today?"

"Monday, sir," said Paris.

"Well then, what about Thursday? What do
you think, my boy?"

"I can hardly wait," said Paris with a smile.

I must be gone and live, or stay and die.

On the balcony, Juliet was saying
goodbye to Romeo. "It's too soon,"
she said. "I wish you could stay,
but you must be safe. Write to
me whenever you can. Will we
really see each other again?"
"I'm sure of it, my love," said Romeo.
The nurse called to her, "Juliet, hurry!
Your mother is coming!"
Juliet kissed Romeo one last time, and
he climbed down from the balcony. Juliet
went slowly back into her room.

"Juliet, are you still awake – and crying again? Crying won't bring Tybalt back, you know," said her mother.

Juliet turned to one side. "I miss him so much!"

"Well, let's give you a reason to be happy. You're going to marry Paris in three days' time."

"Three days? No! It's too soon!"

I will not marry yet.

Juliet's father came in. "Are you questioning me, girl? You know I've always wanted to find a good husband for you." Juliet tried to persuade him, but she only made him angrier. "You'll marry Paris on Thursday, or leave this house and never come back!"

"Mother, please!"

"Do as your father tells you," answered Lady Capulet coldly. Her parents left the room, and Juliet turned to her nurse.

"What shall I do?"

"Well, Romeo has gone, and he can't come back to Verona. Paris would be a very good husband. I think you should marry him."

"I can't do that! Oh, you're no help. I'll go to Friar Laurence. He'll have better advice."

Friar Laurence had a visitor already. "On Thursday? Are you sure?" he asked Paris.

"It's her father's idea. She needs to forget about Tybalt's death, and this wedding will help her," Paris explained.

Juliet came in. "Look, here she is now," said Paris. "Dear wife, I'm glad to see you, but please don't spoil your pretty face with crying."

Happily met, my lady and my wife.

"I'm not your wife yet," said Juliet. "Please, I need to spend some time alone with the friar."

"To talk about your wedding? Yes, of course," said Paris. He kissed her hand, and Juliet looked away. "Until Thursday, my sweet."

He left, and Juliet started crying again. Friar Laurence put a hand on her arm. "I understand, my dear. I honestly don't know what to do."

"I won't marry him!" said Juliet. "I can't! I'd rather die!"

"Hush!" Friar Laurence said gently. "If you're ready to die, perhaps there is something we can try. Take this." He gave her a small bottle. "Go back to your parents, and tell them you've changed your mind."

"Pretend to get ready for the wedding," said the friar, "then drink this the night before. It will make your face pale and your body cold. You'll seem to stop breathing. For almost two days, you'll seem dead, but actually you'll be in a deep sleep. Your family will put you in the Capulet tomb. I'll send a message to Romeo, and we'll come to the tomb. We'll be there when you wake up, so that Romeo can take you back to Mantua. Are you brave enough for that?

Juliet's eyes were shining. "Yes, dear Friar. Thank you!"

L ord Capulet was making arrangements for the wedding. He was giving orders to the servants. "Juliet, where have you been?"

"Father, I'm sorry. I've thought about it. I'll marry Paris – tomorrow, if you say so."

"Good girl!" said Capulet. "Yes, tomorrow, why not? I'll send a message to Paris. He'll be happy!"

"Nurse, help me to choose clothes for the wedding," said Juliet. "Then leave me on my own for the night. I'm sure Mother needs your help."

So please you, let me now be left alone.

When the nurse had gone, she looked at the bottle. "What if it doesn't work? Or what if it works too well, and kills me? No, I daren't think that… but I'll wake up in the tomb, with all the dead people around – and Tybalt's body! Will Tybalt's ghost be there?

Romeo, I'll do this for you." She drank from the bottle, and lay down on her bed.

"Wake up, my sweet!" Juliet's nurse came into the room. "Paris is waiting for you! Juliet? Juliet!" she screamed.

Juliet's parents hurried into the room. "What's this noise?"

"Dead, my lord and lady!"

"Impossible!" "Oh, my child, my only child!"

Help, help! Call help!

Laughing turned to crying in the Capulet house, and Paris sat with his head in his hands. Not long after, they brought Juliet out of her bedroom, and carried her slowly to her funeral at the Capulet tomb.

In Mantua, Romeo had slept late. His servant had ridden to Verona and back already. "What's the news?" Romeo asked. "Did you see Friar Laurence?"

"Sir, I don't know how to tell you. Juliet is dead. The Capulets were taking her to the family tomb. I saw the friar there, but I couldn't speak to him."

"Dead? It's not possible! Get my horse ready, then. I'm going back to Verona, for the last time."

After the servant left, Romeo went to
an old house in a narrow street. A thin,
anxious-looking man came to the door.

"I've come to buy your strongest poison,"
said Romeo.

"Sir, you know I can't sell you that. It's
against our law."

"I'll pay good money – anything you want,"
said Romeo.

The man spoke quietly. "This is the one,
then. It would kill the strongest of men." He
looked unhappy, but he took Romeo's money.

"Juliet, I'll soon be with you – forever,"
said Romeo.

"Friar John!" Friar Laurence was relieved to see the younger man. "Did you find Romeo?"

"I couldn't leave Verona, sir. The guards stopped me at the gate. They knew that I'd visited a sick family recently, and they were afraid that I'd take the sickness with me to Mantua."

"I don't believe it! Juliet will wake soon, and there isn't time to send another message to Romeo. I'll go to the tomb myself. I must get there before Romeo hears the news."

Someone else was at the tomb already. Paris had brought summer flowers. "Flowers as beautiful as you were, my Juliet. I'll come back every night with more," he said, putting them around her body. Then he saw a light, and heard a noise. "Who's this – Romeo? Tybalt's killer? Stop, you!" he shouted, and took out his sword.

"Don't try to stop me, whoever you are," said Romeo. "I don't mean to hurt anyone except myself."

"You shouldn't be here, Montague." Paris attacked, and Romeo fought back. Paris fell down, groaning. "I'm dying, Romeo. At least let me rest with Juliet."

"Paris?" Romeo could see his attacker clearly now. "You loved Juliet, too. There was no reason for you to die." He carried Paris's body and set it down gently, close to Juliet's.

"Oh my dear love, even death hasn't taken away your beauty. I'll never leave you now. One last kiss, and we'll be together forever." He drank the poison. "It's quick, just as the man said. Forever in death, my darling."

Thus with a kiss I die.

Juliet opened her eyes and smiled. "Romeo, did I hear your voice?" She looked beside her, and screamed. "Romeo, what's in your hand? Poison? Oh, didn't you leave any for me?" She put her arms around him, crying.

"Juliet!" Friar Laurence was calling from outside the tomb. "Come out from that terrible place. Let me help you!"

Juliet had found Romeo's knife. "You've left me this, at least. I have the perfect home for it." She stabbed herself and fell, bleeding, on to Romeo's body.

There was a huge crowd outside the tomb by
the time the Prince arrived. Friar Laurence
explained about the marriage and Juliet's plan.

"We are all punished," the Prince said. "You
have lost your son and your daughter, and
I have lost my two young cousins."

Capulet held out his hand to Montague.
"Our quarrel is over," he said.

Montague took his hand. "We'll never
be enemies again. This is the best way to
remember our children. Romeo, Juliet,
forgive your families. We will never
forget you."

O brother Montague, give me thy hand.

About Shakespeare

William Shakespeare lived in London over 400 years ago. Around that time, many new playhouses had recently opened, and they were very popular. Even Queen Elizabeth I went to see Shakespeare's plays. For ordinary people, the plays weren't expensive if you watched them standing up.

Shakespeare often used much older stories in his plays. The story of Romeo and Juliet was known in Italy around sixty years before Shakespeare wrote his play, and it probably came from several much earlier stories. *Romeo and Juliet* soon became one of Shakespeare's most popular plays, and it still is today.

No one is completely sure what Shakespeare looked like. This picture comes from a book of Shakespeare's plays from 1623. It brings together 36 of his plays, including *Romeo and Juliet*, *Hamlet* and *A Midsummer Night's Dream*.

Activities

The answers are on page 48.

The story begins

Can you put these pictures and
sentences in the right order?

A.

He kissed her hand.

B.

"Rosaline's the most
beautiful girl in Verona."

C.

"Put your masks on, boys."

D.

"This quarrel must stop."

E.

"It's time for you to
get married."

F.

"How dare they come here?"

Who's who?

Find *two* sentences that describe
each character.

Romeo...   Juliet...   Tybalt...

A.
...doesn't want
to marry Paris.

B.
...uses herbs to
make medicines.

C.
...kills Mercutio.

D.
...brings a message
to Romeo.

E.
...says Juliet is
old enough to
get married.

F.
...has to leave
Verona.

Friar Laurence...   Lady Capulet...   Juliet's nurse...

G.
...finds Juliet dead (she thinks) in her room.

H.
...has a balcony outside her room.

I.
...tells Romeo not to lose hope.

J.
...buys poison in Mantua.

K.
...says Romeo must not live.

L.
...dies in the street.

Which one is true?

Choose a sentence for each picture.

1.

   A. Juliet was expecting Romeo to be in the garden.

   B. Juliet was surprised that Romeo was in the garden.

2.

   A. Romeo had stayed out all night after the party.

   B. Romeo had gone straight home after the party.

3.

   A. Romeo killed Tybalt.

   B. Mercutio killed Tybalt.

4.

   A. Juliet was crying because Tybalt was dead.

   B. Juliet was crying because Romeo had gone.

A tragic end

Choose a word from the list to finish each sentence.

1.

He gave her a .... bottle.

2.

"I'll wake up, with all the
.... people around."

3.

"Get my horse ...."

4.

Paris had brought ....
flowers.

5.

"We'll be .... forever."

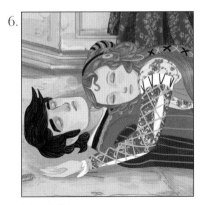

6.

She fell, ..., on to
Romeo.

asleep

bleeding

calm

confused

dead

living

miserable

ready

small

summer

suspicious

together

Word list

balcony (n) a small space outside a door or window in the upper part of a building, with a wall around it.

breathe (v) to take in air through your nose or mouth. You need to breathe to stay alive.

Count (n) a type of lord who is almost as important as a prince.

dull (adj) if something is dull, it is boring and ordinary.

forgive (v) if you forgive someone, you stop being angry that they have done something wrong.

friar (n) a man who lives a very simple life, praying to God and helping other people.

funeral (n) the ceremony after a person has died.

groan (v) when you groan, you make a noise to show that you are feeling pain or you are very unhappy.

hardly (adv) if you can hardly do something, you almost can't do it at all.

hath an old-fashioned way of saying 'has'.

herb (n) a plant that is used in cooking and medicines.

horrified (adj) very shocked.

mask (n) you wear a mask to hide your face, for example at a party or in a play.

mean to (v) if you mean to do something, you want to do it and you plan to do it.

nurse (n) a woman who takes care of a sick person or a small child. In the play, Juliet's nurse is still her servant although Juliet is almost grown up.

on my own alone, without anyone else.

playhouse (n) a special building where actors perform plays.

poison (n) a kind of food or drink that makes you very sick or kills you.

pretend (v) when you pretend, you make someone believe something that isn't true.

punish (v) if you punish someone, you make them pay in some way for doing something wrong.

quarrel (n) a serious argument or disagreement.

spoiled (adj) when something is spoiled, it is no good because it has been damaged.

stab (v) to hurt someone badly or even kill them with a knife or sword.

startled (adj) surprised, particularly by a sound or sudden movement.

'tis an old-fashioned way of saying 'it is'.

thus an old-fashioned way of saying 'in this way'.

thy an old-fashioned way of saying 'your'.

tomb (n) something like a stone house for the bodies of dead people.

Answers

The story begins
D, B, E, C, F, A

Which one is true?
1. B
2. A
3. A
4. B

Who's who?
Romeo – F, J
Juliet – A, H
Tybalt – C, L
Friar Laurence – B, I
Lady Capulet – E, K
Juliet's nurse – D, G

A tragic end
1. small   2. dead
3. ready   4. summer
5. together   6. bleeding

 You can find information about other Usborne English Readers here:
www.usborneenglishreaders.com

Designed by Hope Reynolds
Series designer: Laura Nelson Norris
Edited by Jane Chisholm
With thanks to Andy Prentice
Digital imaging: John Russell

Page 40: engraving of William Shakespeare © Universal History Archive/UIG via Getty Images

First published in 2018 by Usborne Publishing Ltd.,
Usborne House, 83-85 Saffron Hill, London EC1N 8RT, England.
www.usborne.com Copyright © 2018 Usborne Publishing Ltd.